For Mom and Dad
For always making us feel safe and loved…
no matter where,
no matter when,
no matter what.

Thank you for helping us give back one book at a time.
By purchasing this book, you have directly supported:

From the Little Library of

COMMUNITY SPEECH
S E R V I C E S

&

READ MORE DO GOOD ~ READ MORE DO GOOD ~ READ MORE DO GOOD ~ READ MORE DO GOOD ~

Read
FOR A
Cause

There was once a turtle, little and kind,
who went for a walk to pass the time.

He first saw Bird in his nest in a tree...
tucked in the branches,
safe as can be.

"**CAW CAW!**" said Bird.
"Come look at my nest!
My home really is the best of the best!"

Little Turtle sighed
as he plodded ahead,
"I *do* wish I lived there
instead."

He next saw Cow in a barn on a farm.
It was filled with chickens, hay, and charm.

"**MOO MOO!**" said Cow.

"Isn't my place fine?"

"Don't *you* wish you had a
home like mine?"

Little Turtle nodded...
he had to agree.
That barn was better
than any he'd seen.

Little Turtle began to feel
kind of sad…

He wanted homes like his
other friends had.

But Little Turtle had more
friends to see.
So off he went to find
Bear and Bee.

"BUZZ BUZZ!" said Bee.
"Don't mind the mess!"

"We're busy making honey... no time to rest!"

And "**GRRRR!**" said Bear
from his den next door.

"Isn't this great?
Who could ask
for more!"

Little Turtle was now in total despair.
His friends were so lucky—it just wasn't fair.

He wanted to stop and let his heart ache,
But he still had one more stop to make.

"OOH OOH!"

Big Gorilla thumped in glee.

"Look who has come to visit me!"

"But why does my friend look so blue? Tell me, Turtle, what's bothering you."

So Turtle told Gorilla
about his day
And all of his friends
he'd seen on the way.

"I wish I lived in a
nice place too...
Like a barn or a cave
or a hive, don't you?"

Gorilla just laughed
and shook his head:

"You already do,
my friend!" he said.

"Your shell is your home,
and a great one at that.
Wherever you go,
it's there on your back!"

"A home's not about
looks or size,
you see…
It's about feeling

SAFE AND LOVED

as can be."

"My nest, for example, is no grand sight,
And I move and remake it every night."

"But it's still my
favorite place to be,
Because it is perfect and
made just for me."

"Wow," said Turtle, "now I know!
Our homes are with us wherever we go."

"Whether it be a shell or a nest,
As long as it's loved,
it will be the best!"

Little Turtle was happy
and full of pride…
His shell was the best,
not something to hide!

"Thank you, Gorilla,
for setting me straight...

We should do something
to celebrate!"

"How 'bout
a sleepover?"
Little Turtle said.
"You don't even have
to make me a bed!"

Gorilla laughed and the
two snuggled tight,

Dreaming of
home sweet home
all night.

Read for a Cause promotes childhood learning and charitable giving. A portion of every title's sale proceeds is donated to a deserving non-profit organization who embodies the values our books seek to inspire. Your purchase has helped support this mission, and for that we are so grateful.

For more information, visit
www.readforacause.org

Made in the USA
Lexington, KY
23 September 2019